Poetry of an Angst Ridden Teen

Amber Casteel

DEDICATION

To my friends and family

CONTENTS

ACKNOWLEDGMENTS

Shontay, Rae, and Ren

You ladies have really shaped the woman I am now. You guys will remember a lot of these and the mental trauma that goes with them. You guys have helped me so much to get my mind in a better place and my heart at a more peaceful place.

1 SIMPLE

Gentle caresses of light,

A flicker of the small flames.

Memories of the good days,

Good days

The days where I could go on.

Just move on.

Things were not what they seemed

A candle was a magnificent sight.

Lights out, lights out

Teleport me to the days,

My memories tell the stories

Good night, my love

We will walk the playground,

The days when I would push you

Off the swing,

A kiss was the most healing.

Wake up, wake up

The Nightmare has begun.

Let the blood flow

What have I done?

The gentle flames turned to an inferno,

As our innocents was shredded away,

Our world has fell apart. The abyss has been closing in.

Simple, simple

No one see

I promise. I promise

A kiss turned to something

More.

Our innocent minds can't

Comprehend.

Here we are look

Now.

Awaken from the grave.

Look at us now.

A simple touch,

Has me reeling

A simple kiss

Has me wanting.

Looking at what history

Has created.

An early grave for an

Innocent soul.

I learned much too soon,

Too soon for repenting,

A long life to deal with

The memories.

Blood flowing so freely.

Across the play ground

Many years ago.

Too late to repent now.

Please Forgive me

Although I see your pain in your eyes,

I act as if I don't see,

Can it be?

My love you know,

I will always love you,

You were my first.

Forgive me dear.

I am evil.

Can't see what I have done?

I have forced you to watch,

To watch me live.

When every day, you are wasting away.

You lived once, but look at us now

I finally live in the shadows of pain.

Inerasable

It may be best for our memories

To cease.

To waste away.

For today is a new day.

A day, where I have lost

My sanity.

Sanity that kept me settled.

Settled into a life of happiness.

I do things that make you

Ashamed,

Ashamed of me.

I put up my masks so no one sees.

Sees the insanity deep inside,

The voice seems to get louder.

Louder and more noticeable.

Words I can't stand.

They have taken me over

Made me do horrible things.

I don't like their lips,

Their touches.

So please forgive me

Although, I see the pain in your eyes

I still act as if I don't see,

Can it be?

2 I DON'T UNDERSTAND WHY

I don't understand why,
I don't ask why,
Just leave me be,

Me, what a wonder.
I am in constant pain.
A pain that never goes away.

Do you know what
It feels like,
To wake in the middle
Of the night.

In, the middle of the night,
Just to writhe.
Just to be reminded
Of the past and present failures.

Lonely, even when
I am in a crowd.
I feel like nobody sees
Me.

The real,
Weak,
I know that is true.
The tears down my face are proof.

I feel vulnerable now.
I lost someone that saw
Through my masks.
A pup, a baby.

I lost my home.
What did I do wrong?
Was it just that simple?
No, a lifetime of wrongs.

Wrongs; that created
A monster.
A lustful, corrupting
Monster.

I don't understand,
I don't ask why,
Just leave me be.
I could crumble at your fingers.

3 TEARS

The Liquid running down

My face is like a poison,

Running from my eyes.

Memories are like a movie

Running in front of my eyes to

Be miserable.

But I love them with all my

Heart.

My heart has been broken.

Shattered,

How does something like this heal?

Maybe a kiss,

Maybe time.

The only thing keeping

Me alive;

Poetry of an Angst Ridden Teen

It all gets better with time.

Better with time.

It hasn't gotten better yet.

You shattered my heart and

It hasn't gotten better yet.

Just give me the time, girl.

I liked you enough

For tears to cascade

Down my face.

4 YOU WERE SUPPOSED TO BE A NIGHTMARE.

I wish I didn't have this pain,
An undeniable ache.
Hunny, you cannot help the
Helpless.

The pain grows with every tear,
You think I don't care but
Look me in the tear stained eyes.

Do you not understand,
I love you.
I don't know why,
I thought my heart was lost.
So, I guess it's safe to say.
You thawed my frozen
Heart.

O does this mean I will
Pay for what I care for.
I hoped you could be my
Angel.
But everything I regret
My heart.

My heart was frozen
I melted to fast.

Can it be freezing again?
Maybe I will be numb again.
Or my heart will be to shattered to freeze,
To save.

Not caring anymore
Is certainly a delightful
Mask.
A mask that would save
Me from your rejection.

You are certainly a master
Of pain.
You didn't even give me a
Chance.

You are a fascinating
Young woman.
Such darkness,
Yet so bright.

You seem to despise
Everything around you
But still respect it.
You could have never
Known how quickly I
Started to care for
You.

A master at rejection,
I wish I could have
At least tried for you.

Bu on the heart breaking
Day
You disappeared as if
You were a lucid dream.
You were supposed to be
A nightmare.

5 I AM NOT.....

Sometimes I wonder if this is worth
It.
This feeling of numb.
I just don't know
The throbbing and ach of my
Chest. It's all most unbearable.
I am worthless.
I don't deserve the good that you give
Me.
I don't appreciate it so why give
I am a terrible, a worthless
Brat.
I crave your attention
Attention I don't disserve.
Take it away
I am not an angel.
I am not your prince.
I am evil.
I am a mortal.
One day I will die.
Leave you behind.
I will go to the hell
You imagine.
Your innocent soul shall

go on to your personal
Heaven.
I am sorry.
I have always
failed you.
M'dear.

6 DO YOU CRY AT NIGHT?

Do you cry at night?
Just know that I'm crying with you.
No, not next to you.
But yes crying.

Crying with my face next to
my pillow.
Crying even when I didn't want to
Simply crying

Why does your heart ache?
Why does your life seem to
Be a constant struggle?
no question shall be asked.

But tonight, why cry?
Cry because you know I care
Cry because you know I'm crying too.

Simply cry.
Let it all out.
Beat the pillow beneath you.
Silently scream.

At night, long after I fall asleep.
Are you still asleep?

Still crying.
Is that why my nightmares are killing me?

At the demon's hour,
I am crying.
I am awake
Haunted by a presents.

Not good
Not evil
Just simply watching,
Observing.

And if I die tonight,
Remember I cried with you.
I admit my weakness,
Now dear.

Let it out.
I won't ask why
Just cry
How do you cry at night?

7 EVOLUTION

Day turns to night.
Summer turns to fall.
Love turns to hate.
Happiness turns to depression.

Nothing ever remains.
Time evolves,
People change.
Memories fade.

Emotions, oh the marvel.
Some make you feel accepted
Yet, most time leave you feeling
Alone.

In a crowd of thousands
There is always one.
One different from all
Feels different from all

Marvels of uncertain society.
A group afraid of change.
That is why so many die
Murder, oh my.

Blood running through
Dark streets.

A lost voice.
Someone different.

Knives, guns, poisons
Every wall has a story.
Death to all of them.
Not an innocent place.

Innocents, an oblivious
Mind.
Children with ignorance
Running, playing, caring

Growing up to be
Like their fearful adults.
But, yes, with new ideas.
Evolution.

But fearful of elderly
Discrimination.
Why evolution is so
slow.

8 ALIVE

As the blade sinks in,
as the pain hits.

I will not cry.
I will not scream.

I will not let you see my pain.
I will not die with dignity.

You will not miss me.
Please don't miss me.

Every scare is a reminder of
That day,

A day of pain and realization.
today is a new day.

A day of loneliness,
Memories never cease.

The pain never left,
Even when you did.

Your tears stained my shirt.
My screams eased your torment.

Here I am alive.
Alive, alone

My oh my
How you died that day.

You begged me to save you.
Yet, I could not.

Even if you never
Read this

I won't care
You are my past.

Somebody I used to know,
Used to know

My memories of you
Never cease.

You're not alone
In your torment,

Torment anyone
Cold, but alive

9 ACHES

I don't know why but my heart aches.
Aches.
I used to love with all my being.
You exposed me.

My inner monster.
Hurt and alone
Now I have my mind games
Games in which hurt even
The ones I do care for.

Is that all you wanted?
All you worked so hard to do,
To change me.
Now you have it.

Are you proud of me now?
You would be the only one
Even I know I am a mistake.
A horrible mistake.

Aches,
I can't get through a day.
Without being a horrible person.
I hurt myself when I don't
Even realize it.

I wake in tears.
Tears burn.
I am weak
Weak

You always said so
Everyday
You said so.
You said so.

Aches
Every kiss
Aches
Every lie
Aches

Are you proud?
We both have our
Faults
Where are you now?

You changed me,
You left me
I'm left to fight
Fight the new demons.
Blind demons

10 UNTITLED

Pain or lust
Trust or trustless
My memories of emotions are over-
Whelming.
I remember the love.
I remember the pain,
I remember the sweet taste
Of your lips.
Cotton candy was never a
Taste I liked.

Sugar, sweet lips.
Your eyes were daggers.
Daggers that dug into my flesh.
Dug until they found what,
They were looking for.
The anger that was deep within.
Now what are you searching
For?
I have nothing left to offer.

Each hit rang loud and clear.
Those are things I remember well.
Forceful kisses and late night
Curiosity.
But it seems every night ended in tears.
I seem to remember the tears well.

After every experience.
Someone cried.
Past was thrown on the table.

We know each other more than
Anyone else.
But it seems we have changed.
I was the 'man' of your dreams.
You just simply didn't know it.
Now, my addictions have taken over.

ABOUT THE AUTHOR

Amber Casteel was born on January 3rd 1997 in Murfreesboro, Tennessee. She graduated from Community High School and even attended Motlow Community College for two semesters for Studio Arts. Amber has been writing gay erotica since 2008. She has stories posted for free on fanfiction.net using the pin name Brokenheartsandtears. Amber also Posts her rough drafts of possible new books on Wattpad under the username Broken9669.